Lagos Teens and the marketplace of dreams

Dandy Ahuruonye

Published by Dandy Ahuruonye, 2023.

LAGOS TEENS AND THE MARKETPLACE OF DREAMS

First edition. October 5, 2023.

ISBN: 979-8223364900

Written by Dandy Ahuruonye.

Also by Dandy Ahuruonye

THE WHISPERING POET: An Anthology of Igbo And Other
Proverbs
Grocc-ofly
Reading Glasses for Mama Eagle
The Cute Kids of Madugascar
Nora never gave up
A Fishhook and the Riverboy
Positive Brainwash
Groccolli
The Adventures of Groccolli
Happyville
Oh, What a Mars!
Stinky and The Dung Beetle
The Gull Who Must be Obeyed
THE SHOEMAKER: Principles & Guide for Professionals
The Groccolli Pictureland Chatbook
Finding Love in Cahersiveen
Trillion-Her
Lagos Teens and the marketplace of dreams

Watch for more at https://wordpress.com/home/
dandyahuruonye.wordpress.com.

To Ransford and Myrtle Lewis, Streatham, London.

DANDY AHURUONYE

LAGOS TEENS

AND THE MARKETPLACE OF DREAMS

LAGOS TEENS
and
The Marketplace of Dreams

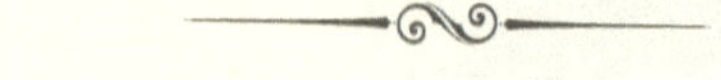

DANDY AHURUONYE
The Whispering Poet

MANY, MANY THANKS

To Ransford and Myrtle Lewis, Streatham, London.

DANDY AHURUONYE

The Whispering Poet

LAGOS TEENS

and

The Marketplace of Dreams

We live in a world where some of our pets are better schooled than some of our children

A Lifetime of Tales from The Whispering Poet

ACKNOWLEDGMENTS

With artistic drawings by De Juvenyles
dandyahuruonyebooks.com

STARTER

Once upon a time, in the bustling city of Lagos, two little hearts beat as one. Tunde and Amina met during their teenage years in a vibrant and crowded market.

They realised they shared common passions for music, art, and freedom as they got to know each other. Above all, they shared a deep and mutual love for each other. But how were they going to successfully and safely navigate the heat of romance while still in their teen years?

One resolution that helped the kids a lot was that Amina and Tunde respected each other's boundaries and values and kept their promise to remain clean and chaste during their relationship.

In this unique book, experience a tale of love, bravery, and devotion as you follow the enthralling journey of two darlings who dared to chase their hearts' desires despite the obstacles and norms that hindered them. Embark on their quest to see if their affection can endure the challenges that come their way. Get into the heart of the tale to see how Amina and Tunde followed their dreams and goals, and how they supported each other in their education and careers.

This is a gripping story of how two youngsters enjoyed hobbies and passions, and how they shared books and movies that helped them to know each other better.

We'll now present a story that will inspire all youths to love wisely and well and to enjoy the rewards of true, unadulterated love in their life. This is a story that will make you smile, cry, laugh, and think. Find out the answer to the question: How were the teens able to find each other in Africa's most populous city? Did they live happily ever after as a married couple? And will they ever overcome all the megacity odds and find happiness together? This is a story that you will never forget; it is the love story of Amina and Tunde: The inexperienced marketplace sweethearts of Lagos.

THE CITY AND A
GIRL'S DREAM

In this first chapter, we'll join Amina in her fateful journey to the Market. Come with her as she wonders about love, and how that simple trip to the market changed her life–forever.

"Amina, my dear, I need you to go to the market and buy some groceries for us. We are running low on rice, beans, tomatoes, and onions. And don't forget to get some fish for the soup." Latifa, Amina's mother, said as she handed her a list and some money.

"Alright, Mama. I'll be back soon," Amina replied, taking the list and the money. She put on her headscarf and sandals, grabbed a basket, and then took off towards the local market in Agege, Lagos.

"Be careful, Amina. The market is very crowded and noisy. Don't let anyone cheat you or take advantage of you. And don't talk to strangers," Latifa shouted the warning, even though she was already on her way. But she heard her and, raising her voice, she responded, "Don't worry, Mama. I know how to handle myself. I've been to the market many times before." Amina's response was a reassurance to her mother, who muttered to herself, "Good girl," but she couldn't help adding, "And hurry back. I need to cook dinner soon so your father, who's just returned home from work, can eat." But somehow, Amina still heard her from several metres away, so she said, "Yes, Mama."

Moments later, she turned and ran back to the house as she had forgotten the bag that her mother gave her for carrying the foodstuff she was going to buy. Latifa eyed her as if to say, "Oh, this is your fortunate day for not forgetting the bag; otherwise, you would have had to carry everything in your headscarf." She kissed her mother on the cheek and headed for the door.

"Bye, Amina. Have a good time at the market." Bola, Amina's father, said as he saw her leaving. He was sitting on the sofa, reading a newspaper and relaxing after a long day's work.

"Bye, Papa. I'll be back soon." Amina said. She smiled at her father and waved goodbye.

The girl stepped out of the apartment and walked down the street. She could hear the sounds of the city: the honking of cars, the shouting of vendors, the laughter of children. Kids like her loved living in Lagos, Nigeria's largest and most vibrant city. It was full of life and energy.

She reached the bus stop and waited for a bus that would take her to the market, but she didn't have to wait long because a yellow bus with black stripes soon arrived. The place was packed with people, but Amina squeezed in and paid the fare; she then found a small seat near the window.

Amina looked out and watched the city pass by. Along the street, there were tall buildings, colourful billboards, busy side streets, and people of all kinds: men in suits, women in dresses, children in uniforms, old people in traditional clothes. The girl felt a sense of wonder and curiosity about them all. Then she wondered what their lives were like, what their dreams and stories were.

It was right at that moment, and for the very first time in her young, busy life, that Amina wondered if she would ever meet somebody one day; someone who would share her life, her dreams, and her own story with her. Such a thought that suddenly crept into her mind was a clear sign that She was now growing into a woman. She wondered if she would ever fall in love.

The teen had never been in love before and had never had a boyfriend or even a crush of any kind. She was too shy and too busy with school and helping her family; she was just like thousands of other young girls scattered all over Lagos who didn't have time for romance or any such luxury.

But now and then, Amina wished she did. She wished she could experience what it was like to have someone else, apart from her parents, who cared for her deeply, made her laugh, and perhaps held her hand. Amina even wished she could experience what it was like to have somebody who would kiss her softly. She has heard stories about youngsters who had feelings of butterflies in their stomachs, sparks in their eyes, and warmth in their hearts and she wondered what it was like to experience such sensations. She would now like to find someone who would make her happy; perhaps someone like Tunde. She didn't know it yet, but she was about to meet him at the market and he was about to change her life — forever! The bus arrived at the market and the girl got off, and like everyone else, followed the crowd into the large open space where hundreds of stalls were set up. The market was full of sights, sounds, smells, and all sorts of foodstuffs spread out attractively in front of several tables that filled the busy street.

A FISHY ROMANCE IN A MARKET

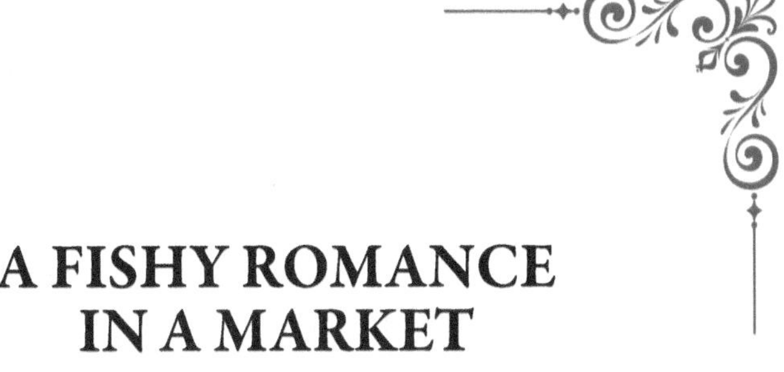

This section deals with a fishy encounter and tells how Amina and Tunde met and fell in love at a busy market. Their story is a romantic comedy involving fish soup and human chemistry. Join the two teens to see how they found each other even in a crowded marketplace, the market of love; love in Lagos Lagoon

Amina approached one display where assorted dried fish were being sold and asked the seller for the price of two portions of smoked salmon.

"Good choice," he said confidently. "Those are the best smoked salmon in this market, and I can sell them to you for N500."

As she contemplated whether that was a fair price or not, a voice suddenly said, "That's not a fair price at all. That's a rip-off; actually, a scam."

Amina turned to her side to see a young man who was also looking to buy fish from the same stall. He then turned to glance at Amina and smiled at her.

"Hi, I'm Tunde. I couldn't help overhearing your conversation with this seller. He's trying to cheat you. The market price for fish is 300 naira per kilo. Don't let him fool you."

His sudden appearance and intervention surprised Amina. She looked at him and felt a strange sensation in her chest, a feeling she'd never had before, and one that she couldn't explain. The boy was tall and handsome, with a smile that could light up any room. She felt an instant connection with him, even though she didn't know his name or anything about him. Confused, she couldn't help smiling back at him.

"Hi, I'm Amina. Thank you for your help. I appreciate it."

The seller was annoyed by Tunde's interference. He glared at him and tried to defend his price.

"Who are you to tell me how to run my business? This is my stall, my fish, my price. If you don't like it, go somewhere else."

Tunde ignored him and continued to talk to Amina.

"S-So, y-you're looking for some fish for your mother's soup, right? What kind of soup are you making tonight?"

Amina told him about her mother's recipe for fish soup, which was her favourite dish.

"Mama uses tomatoes, onions, peppers, garlic, ginger, and other spices to make the broth, and she would normally add the fish and some vegetables towards the end, and this makes her soup really deadly."

"Oh, my vinegar!" Tunde exclaimed. "That has suddenly made me very peckish."

But she continued and told him more and more about her mum's best soup with such enthusiasm and passion that it made Tunde keenly interested in her; she impressed him a lot. But then, as if she finally realised she'd been talking for so long about her mother's recipe, Amina stopped talking and asked the boy to tell her a little about himself and his family.

So, he related to her about his studies at the local college, and how he was learning engineering and hoping to become an inventor. He told her about his dreams of creating new things that would improve lives and solve problems. To her, he came across as intelligent and ambitious, which made Amina to be more curious; she was slowly becoming attracted to the young man.

Through that unarranged meeting and conversation, it became clear to them that they had a lot in common. For example, they both loved reading books, watching movies, listening to music, and learning new things, they both had big goals and aspirations for the future, and they both had a sense of humour and a sense of adventure and came from responsible families. As the teens chatted, they felt some kind of bond gradually forming between them; it felt like a friendship and a chemistry, a romance. They totally forgot about the seller and the fish and the market and the crowd. They forgot about the time and the place, and the only thing they remembered was each other and the moment. But whether the two innocent kids knew it or not; they were falling in love.

A SIMPLE CHAT AND
A SPARK OF LOVE

It was always about the fish that got away; a bittersweet romance about how two teens found and lost each other all in one day. You could call it a fishy farewell or the market of dreams or whatever, but it's a story of how a simple conversation led to a spark of love. At that initial meeting, their love was just a spur and nothing more.

The teenagers talked and talked some more, unaware of how much time had passed. They were so engrossed in each other that they didn't notice the sun setting, the sky darkening, and the market closing. They didn't notice any of that until they heard a loud voice shouting at them.

"Hey, you two! What are you doing here? The market is closing! Get out of here!" The voice belonged to the seller, who had been waiting for them to finish their conversation and buy his fish. He was angry and impatient, and he wanted them to leave.

Amina and Tunde looked at him and then at each other. They realised that they had been talking for ages and that it was getting late. That made each of them to feel a pang of regret and sadness, knowing that they had to part ways.

Therefore, each quickly got up and apologised to the seller.

"Sorry, sir. We didn't mean to bother you. We were just talking." Amina said.

"Yeah, sorry. We lost track of time. We'll go now." Tunde said.

They turned to leave, but then stopped to look into each other's eyes; it was then that they felt a surge of emotion. Both wanted to say something, to do something, to express what they felt. But they didn't know how.

"Are you both going home without buying the fish? What are you going to tell your parents when you get home empty-handed?"

"You're right, sir! However, your salmon is too expensive," Amina said. Tunde said the same before they turned to each other once more. They were both nervous, unsure of what the other thought or felt. They didn't want to ruin the moment or scare the other away. So, they hesitated, searching for the right words, the right actions, and the right signs; but they found none. Finally, they settled for a smile. They waved and said goodbye.

"Well, I guess this is it; so, I might as well say goodbye to you, Amina. It was nice meeting you. Here, please take this piece of paper. That's my cell phone number in case you decide to text or something like that"

"Me too; bye, Tunde. It was great meeting you too. Here's my number as well; you never know....."

They walked away from each other as they felt a mixture of both happiness and sadness; a sense of hope and doubt, as well as joy and pain, as they weren't sure if and when they might see each other again. They had to walk away, but they couldn't stop thinking about each other. Although Lagos was a big city, they both felt there was a slight chance they might see each other again. True, they separated from each other, but there were signs they were falling in love.

Amina took the bus back to her apartment, hoping her parents wouldn't be angry with her for being late, and that they wouldn't ask too many questions about where she had been or what she had done. Then there was the glow on her face or the sparkle in her eyes; might her mother, who was always observant, pick up on those? Well, she could only hope they wouldn't notice that she was in love.

She reached her apartment, opened the door and saw her mother in the kitchen, cooking dinner. Amina smelled the aroma of fish soup and felt a twinge of guilt. She remembered that she had forgotten to buy the fish for her mother's soup. The young girl wondered how her mother had managed to get it. She greeted her mother with a kiss and an apology.

"Hi, Mama. I'm sorry I'm late. I got stuck in traffic." She lied.

Latifa looked at her daughter and smiled because she was an experienced woman and could see all the signs on Amina's face and body language, it was obvious to her that the girl was lying, but she didn't mind as a mother always knows, she could tell her daughter had met someone; her daughter was in love.

Latifa had seen Amina get off the bus and enter the apartment; the glow on her face and the sparkle in her eyes, the happiness and excitement in her expression and posture. She had seen it all before. The mum remembered seeing the same signs even in herself when she was young, like her daughter; it was the day that Bola and she met for the first time at a wedding. She had seen it in Bola when he was young and proposed to her at a park. Latifa had seen it in them when they were married and had Amina as their daughter. Yes - she had seen love and all its telltale signs.

LATIFA LET HER DAUGHTER have her moment of bliss and not ask too many questions or make too many comments so as not to spoil the mood or dampen the spirit. If anything, she wanted to be happy for her daughter and support her choices. To Amina's surprise, her mum hugged her and accepted her apology.

"It's alright, my dear. I'm glad you're home safe and sound."

She told her daughter that she had bought some fish from another stall when she realised she was running late. Mum told her daughter that dinner was almost ready and that Bola, who had gone out on a little stroll, would be home soon.

"Please go wash upstairs and get ready for dinner. I love you very much."

Amina thanked her mother and did as she was told and buzzed to the bathroom and had a wash and afterwards looked at herself in the mirror and smiled. The girl thought about Tunde and felt a warm sensation in her chest to the point of almost feeling faintish, but she recovered and wondered if he was thinking about her too. Amina then wondered when she would see him again, what next might happen between them, and whether he loved her as much as she loved him.

Tunde took a taxi back to his dormitory and hoped that Femi, his roommate, wouldn't be there or wouldn't bother him and asking him to explain where he'd been or what he had done. Tunde hoped he wouldn't have to explain the fact that he was falling in love.

Arriving at the dormitory, the boy entered his room and saw his roommate on the bed reading. Tunde smelled the scent of pizza and felt a pang of hunger. It was then that the teen remembered that he had eaten nothing since breakfast and wondered, "How on earth had I survived that long without food?" Anyway, he greeted his colleague with a nod and a hello.

"Hey, Femi. What's up?"

Femi looked at him and grinned. He knew he was hiding something, but he didn't know what. But he can tell that he was probably in love.

He had seen him leave the dormitory a while back and was only returning now when it was already evening. Then what about the unmistakable glow on his face and the sparkle in his eyes? He knew because he had seen it all before.

FEMI HAD SEEN IT IN himself when he was dating Nkechi, his girlfriend. So, he teased his roommate and had some fun by asking him questions and making mischievous remarks just to spoil the mood and dampen Tunde's spirit.

"So, where have you been all day, dude? You didn't answer any of my calls or texts."

"I was busy," Tunde said.

"Busy with what? Studying? Working? Sleeping?"

"None of your business,"

"Come on, man. Don't be like that. You can tell me anything, you know; I'm your best friend."

"No, you're not. You're my roommate." Tunde said.

"Same thing. So, spill it. What were you doing?"

Tunde sighed and gave up. From experience, Tunde knew Femi wouldn't give it up unless Tunde gave him an answer, any answer. So, Tunde told him the truth, but not the whole truth. Yes, it would be okay to tell him about Amina; but not about his feelings for her.

"I met a girl at the market and talked to her for a while. She was nice and smart and pretty, and we might meet again. I would say that for now, she's just a friend."

Femi pretended to listen attentively while nodding sarcastically. He knew he was lying, but he didn't mind. He knew more than what he said or showed. His feeling for Amina was clear, and as far as he was concerned, he was in love. Still, he allowed his roommate to have his moment of denial; after all, he must respect his privacy.

"That's great, man. I'm happy for you. She sounds like a nice girl. Anyway, I ordered some pizza for dinner and that there are some left for you if you're hungry. I finished my homework and I'm going to relax a bit now and watch a movie on my laptop."

Tunde thanked him before helping himself with some pizza and felt better. He thought about Amina and wondered if she loved him as much as he loved him.

BACK TO THE
MARKET OF
DESTINY

Let's now look at a love story that continued with a text and led to a second date; but will Amina and Tunde be reunited at the market? They did and their love blossomed with a smile, making this place the market of destiny where Amina and Tunde found each other again and again; the market of love.

It was no coincidence that the next day, both Amina and Tunde woke up with a smile on their faces because they had both dreamt of each other the night before and felt a sudden surge of happiness and couldn't wait to see each other again to continue their conversation.

They checked their phones and saw that they had received a text message from each other; it surprised them to notice that they had both texted each other the same 'good morning' and wished each other a lovely day. Although they were miles apart, they felt a flutter in their stomachs and a warmth in their hearts all at the same time, and the teens continued to text one another; that went on and on as the teens sent text messages back and forth for a while, exchanging compliments, jokes, and emojis. In the end, they agreed to meet again at the same market one afternoon the following week, after they had finished their school and work. They said goodbye and put away their phones.

Soon, the day they had agreed to meet arrived and that morning they got ready and left their homes.

Amina went to her school, where she was a senior student. The girl was smart and hardworking; she desired to go to college and study medicine, which would allow her to become a doctor; she was the kind of girl who would do anything to help people. Her love for learning new things and expanding her knowledge helped her a lot, and that was why she excelled at all subjects, but she especially liked science and math. Amina enjoyed the experiments in science classes that taught her to solve problems and find answers.

Her kindness and generosity meant that she had many friends at school who liked her because she was always willing to help them at those times when they got stuck with their homework. Amina often lent them her notes and shared her snacks. The girl was also popular with the teachers, who praised her for making their job easier because of her diligence and discipline. So, it was no surprise that Amina was happy at school, but these days she was happier when she thought of Tunde, and that was happening very often now; during every class, every break, every moment.

"Who knows what he is doing or what he is thinking and feeling right now," she wondered, "Does he miss me as much as I missed him?"

On the other side of the city, Tunde went about his daily routine at the college. The young man loved creating new things and applying his skills, and enjoyed designing devices, building machines, and testing solutions.

Meanwhile, their parents were also busy with their own lives.

Amina's parents were Latifa and Bola. They were both teachers at a local primary school. They loved teaching young children and helping them grow and learn.

The couple had met when they were both students at the same college and moved to Lagos from their hometowns soon after getting married. They'd been blessed with Amina as their only child; therefore, it was understandable that they loved her more than anything and would do anything to help her be happy in life.

They were proud of her efforts at school and supported her dreams, but they also taught her that it was very important for a young person like her to be humble and grateful for what she had. As parents, Latifa and Bola were always happy, but they were happier when they saw Amina happy. They saw her happiness when she came home from the market the previous day. It showed in her smile, her eyes, and in her voice. It meant only one thing; she had met a boy.

They didn't know much about him, but they trusted Amina's judgement; hoping he was a good lad who would treat Amina well and make her happy. They couldn't wait to meet him and welcome him into their family someday.

Tunde's parents were Shola and Tola, who were both lawyers at a prestigious law firm. They loved practising law and defending justice.

On the day they had arranged the week before, Amina and Tunde met again at the market in the afternoon. Oh, they were both excited about seeing each other again. It was a little awkward at the beginning, but soon, they greeted each other with a hug and a smile; then they went on a walk around the market and explored the different stalls and bought some snacks and drinks from one of the sweet shops and shared them. They talked about their interests, but every once in a while, they laughed at each other's jokes and stories. Things were a bit different now as they felt more comfortable with each other; feeling more connected and attracted to each other.

THIS SECOND MEETING was also an opportunity for them to learn more about each other's families. Amina told Tunde about her parents; that they were teachers at a primary school. She told him how they had met at college and moved to Lagos from the countryside, and how they loved teaching and helping children.

Tunde did not interrupt her at all, but rather, he listened attentively as the girl told him about her parents. Everything she told him fascinated him. Then, it was his turn to tell Amina about his own parents, Shola and Tola.

"My mum and dad are lawyers at a law firm; they met at work and later got married before I came along, and they've lived in Lagos all their lives. I respect them a lot because they're good at their jobs and find lots of satisfaction in defending the poor who need justice."

Now that they've come to know a little more about each other, they suddenly realise that even though their parents had different backgrounds and careers, they still had some things in common. For example, all their parents valued hard work and wanted their children to be successful.

However, the kids were still worried; they hoped that their parents would get along well and approve of their growing relationship. And before they went their separate ways that day, they decided to introduce their parents to each other soon, and that the best way to go about it was to invite them for dinner at Amina's apartment the next day.

"It would be a wonderful opportunity to get to know each other better and have some fun," Amina told him.

"Oh, my deadly! If so, I look forward to seeing their reactions and impressions tomorrow. I'm really excited now," Tunde remarked.

"Before then, why don't you first come with me to meet them? This would make things a bit easier and no one would be shocked when the parents finally meet."

"Oh, slow down here, please; are you trying to put me under the bus? Why don't I take you to come meet my parents instead?"

"C'mon! You're the lad here, so go on and take the heat for me, for us; I promise you, it would be alright. What do you say?"

"I'm not sure if this is a good idea; but if you insist, then I'll come with you."

"You'll see, it will work, come!"

THE TEA OF LOVE

In this section, the story begins with a fish and ends with a family after they receive their parents' approval and how the introduction of both their parents went on to bridge two worlds.

Amina felt a surge of nervousness as she walked into her apartment with Tunde by her side. The youth knew she had to tell her parents about him, but she was not sure how they would react. She hoped they would be understanding and supportive, but she also feared they might be angry or disappointed. She loved Tunde and wanted nothing else than for her parents to love him too and approve of him. Therefore, the girl took a deep breath and opened the door. She saw her mother, Latifa, sitting on the sofa, reading a magazine. Her father, Bola, was in the kitchen, preparing some tea. They both looked up and smiled when they saw their daughter.

"Hello, darling. How was your day?" Latifa asked.

"It was good, Mum. I have someone I want you to meet," Amina said, gesturing to Tunde.

"Who is this handsome young man?" Bola asked, coming out of the kitchen with a tray of tea and biscuits.

"This is Tunde. He's my friend," Amina said, hoping her voice did not betray her nervousness.

"Hello, Tunde. It's nice to meet you." Latifa said, getting up and shaking his hand.

"Hello, madam, it's nice to meet you too," he said politely.

"Please, call me Latifa. And this is my husband, Bola." Latifa said, introducing her husband.

"Hello, sir. I'm pleased to meet you," Tunde said, shaking his hand.

"Please, call me Bola; we're not that formal around here," Bola said, smiling warmly.

"PLEASE, SIT DOWN AND join us for some tea," she said, inviting them to the sofa.

"Thank you," Tunde said, sitting next to Amina.

Amina felt a wave of relief as she saw her parents being welcoming to her friend; so she decided to be open and honest with them and tell them the truth about their relationship.

"Mum, Dad, there's something I need to tell you," Amina said, taking Tunde's hand in hers.

"What is it, dear?" she asked, sensing her seriousness.

"Tunde and I are more than just friends. We're in love." Amina said, looking into Tunde's eyes.

There was a moment of silence as Amina's parents processed what she had just said. Her remarks had taken her parents unawares, and it felt like it was taking them an entire year to recover and come up with a response. As she waited for their reaction, Amina felt her heart pounding so violently in her chest as if it was going to burst her ribcage.

Latifa was the first to speak. Surprisingly, she smiled and reached out to hug Amina.

"Oh, Amina, I'm so happy for you; it pleases me that you have now found someone who makes you happy."

Bola too nodded and patted Tunde on the shoulder.

"Yeah, I agree with your mother; I'm happy for you too, son. You seem like a fine young man who cares for my daughter." Bola said.

Amina felt tears of joy in her eyes as she hugged her parents back. She was so grateful that they accepted and supported her choice.

"Thank you so much, Mum and Dad. You don't know how much this means to me."

"We're your parents, Amina. We love you unconditionally, and we want you to succeed in life, to be happy," her mother said.

"As long as you respect each other's boundaries and values, follow your dreams and goals, honour your culture and traditions, and share your hobbies and passions, we have no reason to object to your relationship," Bola added.

Amina smiled and kissed her parents on the cheek.

"You're the best parents ever," she said.

Tunde also thanked them for their kindness and understanding.

"Thank you for welcoming me into your family. I promise I will treat Amina with respect and care."

"We trust you will, Tunde, and we're glad to have you as part of our family too," Latifa said.

AMINA FELT A SURGE of happiness as she cuddled with Tunde on the sofa; she looked and felt like she had everything she ever wanted in life: a loving partner, supportive parents, and a bright future ahead of them. Then, that was a golden moment to take the next step and introduce their parents to each other.

"Mum, Dad, there's one more thing I want to ask you if you wouldn't mind."

"What is it?" Bola asked.

"Tunde's parents are also very nice and supportive of us. They're Shola and Tola. They live in Ikeja. I was wondering if we could invite them over for dinner tomorrow night so that you can meet them and get to know them better."

"That sounds like a lovely idea, sweetheart," Latifa said.

"Yes, we'd love to meet them," Bola approved.

"Great! Thank you so much! Tunde, please call them right away and let them know." Amina asked excitedly.

"Sure."

He took out his phone and dialled his parents' number, and hoped they would be free and willing to come over for dinner.

"Hello, Mum. It's me. I have some good news for you."

Amina could hear the faint sound of Tunde's mother's voice on the other end.

"Hello, Tunde. What is it, son?" Tola asked.

He told her about Amina's parents' invitation and asked if they could come over with him to their house for dinner the next day.

She was delighted and agreed to come.

"That's wonderful, but I'll check with your dad first before confirming."

Overhearing her, Shola confirmed it was okay.

"We'd love to come over and meet her parents, say 'thank you' to them for inviting us."

Tunde thanked them and hung up.

"They said yes! They're coming over tomorrow!" Tunde announced happily.

"That's awesome! I can't wait to see them!" Amina said.

They hugged each other and smiled, and felt like they had taken a huge step forward in their relationship. They looked forward to the next day when they would introduce their parents to each other and hope for the best. The youngsters weren't naïve; they knew it would not be easy, but they also knew they must face these types of challenges in life. Well, they had each other, and that was enough. And, after all, they were in love; nothing could stop them now.

THE FEAST FROM SWEETHEARTS

Amina and Tunde cooked for their parents, won their hearts and turned the meal into a feast of joy because they shared their food and their feelings; bringing two families together.

The next day, Tunde left his dormitory early and came over to Amina's place and found her busy preparing for the meal, he quickly joined her because they wanted to make a good impression on their parents and show them how much they had matured and how much they cared for each other. They decided to cook a variety of dishes that represented their different cultures and tastes. They made jollof rice, egusi soup, fried plantain, chicken curry, chapati, and salad. They also baked a chocolate cake for dessert. The teens worked hard to set the table with colourful plates and napkins and decorated the apartment with flowers and candles. They hoped that their parents would enjoy the food as well as the atmosphere.

Soon, they heard a knock on the door around six o'clock and Amina opened it and saw Tunde's parents standing outside. They looked elegant and friendly, wearing traditional outfits. She greeted them very respectfully, smiled at them, and invited them in.

"Hello, Shola and Tola. Welcome to our home; I'm so glad you could come." Amina said.

"Hello, Amina. Thank you for having us. You have a lovely home," Shola said.

"Hello, dear. You look beautiful. And your cooking smells delicious," Tola said, sniffing the air.

"Thank you. That's very kind of you," the young girl replied, blushing a little. She quickly took their coats and hung them in the closet. She then led them to the living room, where her parents were waiting.

"Mum, Dad, these are Tunde's parents, Shola and Tola."

"Hello, Shola and Tola. It's a pleasure to finally meet you." Latifa said, shaking their hands.

"Hello, Latifa and Bola. It's wonderful to meet you too," Shola said.

"Yes, we're happy to meet you," Bola said.

They all sat down on the sofa and exchanged pleasantries while talking about their jobs, their hobbies, their families, and their backgrounds. Both the hosts and the guests found out that they had some things in common, such as their love for music, books, and travel. They also learned about their differences, such as their religions, languages, and customs. They listened to each other with respect and curiosity, trying to understand each other better.

Amina and Tunde watched them from the kitchen, feeling relieved and hopeful. For them, it was absolute bliss to see their parents smiling and laughing, getting along well and enjoying each other's company.

"They seem to like each other," Amina leaned over and whispered to Tunde.

"They sure do," he whispered back.

Amina and Tunde finished cooking the food and brought it to the dining table and then called their parents to join them for dinner.

"Wow, this looks amazing," Shola said, admiring the food.

"And it smells wonderful too," Tola said, salivating.

"Thank you. We cooked it together," Amina told them in a very proud tone.

"We wanted to show you our appreciation for your support and acceptance of our relationship," Tunde said gratefully.

"That's very sweet of you," Latifa warmly responded.

"You're very welcome," said Bola.

Everybody sat down at the table and served themselves some food, complimented each other on their cooking skills and tasted the different dishes. They praised the flavours and textures of the food, expressing their delight and satisfaction.

"Oh, my vinegar!! This jollof rice is wickedly delicious," Latifa couldn't help but say after she had shovelled a spoonful of the tasty rice into her mouth.

"I feel the same, it's one of my favourite dishes, and this one is sooo good," Shola said as he lifted a large piece of smoked catfish from his plate and pushed it into his mouth, and as he tried to munch it down, the fish formed a small lump on his left cheek.

Tola, who liked chicken meat very much, remarked, "This chicken curry is one of the best I've had in a long time; you must share the recipe with me later."

Hearing her husband, Shola added, "Darling, you must try the fried plantain; I can assure you; it is heavenly!"

"Thank you. It's one of Amina's favourites," Latifa said.

Bola then shifted from the jollof rice to the egusi soup. He made a cup with his fingers and scooped some soup into his mouth. After moving the delicacy around in his mouth for a while, he finally exclaimed, "This egusi soup is delightful; I love it. You must make this again, as I'm having the best time."

"Oh, thank you. It's one of Tunde's favourites." Tola said.

They continued to eat and talk, sharing stories and jokes, and making compliments. Everyone felt relaxed with each other, enjoying the food and the conversation.

Amina and Tunde were overjoyed to see their parents bonding over their cooking; to them, it felt like they had achieved their goal of bringing their families together. They felt like they had made a big step forward in their relationship, too. They cleared the table and brought out the chocolate cake for dessert, and after cutting slices for everyone, they served them with ice cream.

Amina thanked them all and felt tears of joy in her eyes because she felt like she had everything she ever wanted. She looked at Tunde and caught him smiling at her. He came over to her to hold her hand and squeezed it gently. He leaned in and whispered in her ear.

"I'm so happy to have you, my love; you're the best thing that ever happened to me. I love you more than words can say."

Amina smiled and kissed him softly while whispering back in his ear.

"Thank you, my love. You're the most amazing thing that ever happened to me, too. I love you more than words can say."

LEARNING FROM
EACH OTHER'S
WORLDS

In this section, we join Amina and Tunde as their love story explores books and movies in an exchange of love that allows them to share their hobbies and passions.

Amina and Tunde's romance was now blossoming into a serious relationship, and there was excitement as they had invited them for dinner at Amina's place and introduced them to each other. The kids were happy to see that, right from their first face-to-face meeting, their parents got along well; then they later gave their approval to their relationship.

The youngsters saw each other more often and spent more time together. They discovered they lived not too far from each other, only a few miles away and so felt it would be nice to go on a walk on some evenings after school to enjoy some fresh air and the scenery. Amina and Tunde were now holding hands and talking about their plans and dreams because they were now feeling more comfortable with each other; more connected and attracted to each other.

As they spent time together on walks, they learned more about each other's hobbies and passions. On one occasion, Amina told him about her love for reading books, especially novels and biographies.

"I like to immerse myself in different worlds and lives, and I spend quite some time admiring the authors who created them. I believe authors are gifted individuals."

Tunde also told Amina about his love for movies, especially sci-fi and action.

"Well, that love you have for books is the same love that I have for movies; I marvel at the special effects and the stunts; they make me wonder and I'm often inspired by the directors who made them.

BOTH OF THEM REALISED they had different tastes and preferences, but they also had some things in common. They both appreciated art and creativity, enjoyed stories and characters, and respected each other's opinions and choices. The next challenge would be for them to learn from each other and grow together, to share those hobbies and passions. To get to know each other even better, the youngsters agreed to exchange books and movies that they liked and recommend them to each other.

"It would be a good way to get to have some fun as well. It would be priceless to see each other's reactions and impressions afterwards," they said.

SHARING LISTS OF AFFECTION

They bonded over stories and characters; discovering new tastes and preferences.

Amina and Tunde exchanged books and movies that they liked and recommended them to each other. They wanted to share their hobbies and passions and learn more about each other's sensitivities and likings. The kids began by giving each other a list of five books and five movies that they thought the other would enjoy and even wrote a brief note for each item explaining why they chose it and what they liked about it.

Amina's list of books for Tunde was:

• The Alchemist by Paulo Coelho. Amina wrote: "This is one of my favourite books, and I like how it focuses on a young man who goes on a journey to find his destiny and his treasure. By reading it carefully, you'll find that it's full of wisdom and inspiration. I hope you like it as much as I do."

• Things Fall Apart by Chinua Achebe: "This is a classic novel by a Nigerian author that looks at the life and culture of an Igbo village before and after the arrival of the British colonialists, and presents a powerful but tragic story that shows the impact of change and history. I think you'll find this one very interesting and relevant."

• The Whispering Poet - An Anthology of Igbo and Other Proverbs by Dandy Ahuruonye: It's a collection of over 600 pages of proverbs from the Igbo culture and other parts of the world, with explanations, illustrations, and parallel applications. The author uses proverbs to explore the wisdom and truth of the human condition and to show the similarities and differences between various worldviews. This volume is not only informative but also entertaining and inspiring. You will learn a lot about the Igbo language, culture, and heritage, as well as other proverbs that can enrich your understanding of the world. I think you'll love this one because it is a rare treasure of ancient and modern wisdom."

• The Little Prince by Antoine de Saint-Exupéry. Amina wrote: "This is a beautiful book that I read when I was a child. It's about a pilot who meets a little prince from another planet. This book is full of imagination, wonder, and wisdom. It's a book for children and adults alike. I hope it makes you smile and think."

• Long Search for Greener Pastures by Dandy Ahuruonye: the life of Chike, a young Igbo man who struggles to make a better future for himself and his family after the Biafra-Nigeria War. The book is a captivating blend of history, culture, and adventure, as Chike travels across Nigeria and beyond, facing various challenges and opportunities. You'll learn a lot about the Igbo language, culture, and heritage, as well as the history and politics of Nigeria. You will also enjoy the humour, romance, and suspense that fill the pages of this novel, as well as the life and struggles of both the ancient and modern Igbo people.

• The Kite Runner by Khaled Hosseini: "This is a moving book that I read recently that talks about the friendship between two boys in Afghanistan; Amir, a wealthy boy from Kabul, and Hassan, the son of his father's servant, who belong to different ethnic and social group. It explores the complex and often painful relationship between the boys, as well as the impact of war, trauma, guilt, and redemption, and how their lives are affected by war, betrayal, and redemption. It's full of emotion, drama, and courage and will definitely touch your heart and soul."

When she finished presenting her list to Tunde, he jokingly confronted her.

"Hey, wait a minute. I thought we agreed to exchange five items; it looks like you've given me six books instead. That's unfair!"

"Ah, c'mon! I gave you six wonderful books, didn't I?"

"But that's cheating because you didn't keep to our agreement."

"Just give them a try sweetheart; I promise you'll thank me later!"

"Old vinegar! That's what you are," he told her as both of them continued to wind each other up and laugh. Then Tunde said, "I can see what you're trying to do; you are planning to make me forget to give you my own list of items, but you've failed miserably. Anyway, here's my list of movies for my beloved Amina:"

• The Avengers by Joss Whedon. "This is one of my favourite movies. It's about a team of superheroes who save the world from an alien invasion. It's full of action and humour, with some special effects that I'm sure you like, just as I did."

• The Lion King by Roger Allers and Rob Minkoff. "Oh, you must watch this one; actually, I recommend that see it first as it is a classic by Disney. The movie is about the life and adventures of a lion cub who becomes the king of the jungle. It's full of music, animation, and emotion throughout."

• The Matrix by Lana Wachowski and Lilly Wachowski is a popular movie series that has been made into games and explores a dystopian world where humans are enslaved by machines in virtual reality. It's full of sci-fi, action, and philosophy. I know you like science and math in it. That's why I think you'll enjoy it."

• The Notebook by Nick Cassavetes. "This is a beautiful movie that I watched with my parents. It's about a love story between a young couple who are separated by war, class, and time. It's full of romance, drama, and nostalgia that makes you smile and cry."

• The Pursuit of Happyness by Gabriele Muccino. "This moving movie that I watched with my friends is about the true story of a man who struggles to provide for his son while pursuing his dream of becoming a stockbroker. The storyline is full of hardship, hope, as well as happiness."

They exchanged their lists and thanked each other for their recommendations, agreeing to read or watch one book or movie every week and discuss it afterwards.

THE CHAPERONS OF
CHASTITY

As their romance gathers strength, Amina and Tunde must choose purity by delaying intimacy until marriage and bringing honour to everyone, including themselves. Read on to find out how the youths avoided potential temptations by waiting for the right time.

Amina's and Tunde's relationship grew stronger and deeper. They had read or watched each other's books and movies and discussed them with each other. They had learned more about each other's hobbies and passions and shared them. After all that, the youths also expressed their love and commitment for each other and to each other. Finally, they said the three words that meant the world to them: 'I love you,' and also felt the joy and peace that came with them when each replied: 'I love you too.' This made each of them thrilled, but they were also determined to be responsible and mature about their growing affection for each other. They knew that love was not just a feeling, but also a choice that also required an action. They reminded one another that love was not just a gift, but also a duty; it required respect, trust, honesty, loyalty, patience, kindness, forgiveness, and, most of all, sacrifice.

Because of their strong parental training, the teens knew too well that a relationship between a boy and a girl required purity and chastity. Those were their reasons for deciding to remain morally clean during their teen relationship, to delay intimacy until they were old enough and married. This will enable them to honour God, themselves, and each other with their bodies, even though that will not be easy. Tunde and Amina made this decision together, after having a serious conversation about their values, beliefs, goals, and expectations. In that open conversation, they also spoke about their fears about what the future holds for them and the challenges that lay ahead.

IN THE END, THE YOUTHS agreed to follow some clear guidelines and boundaries to help them keep their decision and avoid situations that could compromise their immorality.

"Tunde, I want to talk to you about something important."

"Sure, Amina. What is it?"

"It's about us, our relationship."

"Yeah? What about it?"

"Well, you know how much I love you, right?"

"Of course, I do. And you know how much I love you, too."

"Yes, I do. And I'm so happy that we're together. You make me feel so special and cherished."

"Same here. You make me feel proud; I feel secure with you."

"But I also want us to be careful and wise and not do anything that we might regret later, or do something that might hurt ourselves or others."

"I understand what you mean, and I completely agree with you."

"Really? You do?"

"Yes, I do. I've been thinking about this too."

"You have?"

"Yes, I have. And I've come to the same conclusion as you."

"Which is?"

"That we should remain clean and faithful during our teen relationship. That we should delay intimacy until we're married."

"Wow. I'm so glad to hear that. That's exactly what I think too. But how are we going to do that?"

"It's easy; we should always have a chaperon to keep an eye on what we're doing."

"A chaperon? What is that?"

"It is a person who goes with you to a place or an event to make sure you are safe and behave well. For example, one of our parents might be our chaperon to make sure we're not alone, because that's when we could do things we shouldn't do."

"If so, I say 'amen' to that plan."

MUTUAL POEMS OF PURITY

Learning from a wise and firm chaperon stopped Amina and Tunde in their tracks when they almost crossed the line because of passion

Tunde and Amina were in love and wanted to spend more time together and get to know each other better, but also wanted to respect their parents' wishes and follow their culture's norms. They knew they had to wait until they were married to be intimate with each other. But to do so, a guardian must be with them when they went out or visited each other. Tunde and Amina understood the need to be very careful and avoid temptation.

Their supervisor was Bunmi, Amina's aunty, thirty years old and a lawyer. Bunmi was wise and firm, but also fun to be around, and she loved her niece and wanted her to have a happy life. She also loved Tunde and treated him like a nephew. She agreed to be their chaperon because she understood their feelings and their situation.

Bunmi was not a lenient or dull chaperon who ignored and left them to their own devices. No, she was there to help, guide, and protect them by giving them advice, suggestions, and encouragement. The lawyer regularly reminded them of their values and goals, as well as the boundaries they should not cross. This protected the teens as she monitored what they were doing, intervening when necessary, and preventing any potential trouble. Bunmi did all this with honour, making sure to respect their dignity, and employing poetry to make her point to the youths, and they understood she was only trying to guide them.

For example, one day, Tunde and Amina went to her school's end-of-year party, and Bunmi had to go with them but stayed in the background. She let them dance, chat, and have fun with their friends and enjoy the atmosphere, too. However, when the party got too loud and crowded, Bunmi noticed that Tunde and Amina were getting too close and comfortable with each other. She saw them moving to a dark corner of the hall, away from the crowd. She heard them giggling and whispering to each other; Bunmi knew they were about to do something inappropriate and took action to intervene before they crossed the line. The woman walked towards them and tapped them on the shoulder before saying in a firm, poetic voice:

"Children, love is a song
A melody that fills the air
But love is not a simple affair
That flows with no rhyme or aim
Or follows without a season

Love is a dance that moves the feet
But love is also very arranged
And needs a measure and a pace
And not a rush like a chase
Love is a glow for the eyes

But love is also very sensible
And can be seen by everyone
And not be hidden from anyone
Love is a joy that you both feel
But love is also very real

And should be voiced and shown
And not be kept or blown apart

So please be careful and please be alert
And please don't let your love get hurt
By what you do in the hall so dark

Or what you say in the corner so stark
Remember your parents and your faith
And remember your culture and your fate
Remember, your chaperon is here for you
To help you stay safe and stay true"

Tunde and Amina heard Bunmi's words and felt a jolt of panic in their hearts after realising they were about to do something wrong and disrespectful. At once, they moved away from each other and looked around with their heads bent downwards. Yes, the teenagers felt guilty and embarrassed by their behaviour. Still, Bunmi's words made them feel a bit of gratitude in their hearts because, after reflecting on everything that she said, they concluded that she was right and that she cared for them by saving them from making a mistake that could ruin their reputation and their future. Bunmi had reminded them that integrity, honesty, and morality were more important in life than one moment of stolen bliss.

THEY RAISED THEIR HEADS and looked at Bunmi and apologised for their behaviour. Soon, the party was over and they all left together to enjoy the rest of the night without any more incidents. At last, they went back to Tunde's apartment feeling happy and content.

On another day, Tunde and Amina went to the park for a picnic and Bunmi went with them as their chaperon. The lady sat on a bench a few metres away to give them some space so they could talk, eat, and play together and have a little privacy.

However, when the park got less crowded, and the sun started to set, Bunmi noticed that Tunde and Amina were getting too cosy and comfortable with each other. She saw them lying on the grass, cuddling and whispering sweet nothings in each other's ears. It was then she knew they were about to get carried away by their emotions. Once again, Bunmi intervened before they crossed the line. She got up from the bench, walked up to them and sang a memorable, poetic rhyme:

> *"Love is a flower that blooms in the spring*
> *But love is not a simple thing*
> *That grows without care or attention*
> *Or survives without protection*
> *Love is a bird that flies in the sky*
>
> *But love is also very shy*
> *And needs a nest to rest and hide*
> *And not be exposed to the outside*
> *Love is a star that shines in the night*
> *But love is also very bright*
>
> *And can be seen by everyone*
> *And not be hidden from anyone*
> *Love is a gift that you both share*
> *But love is also very rare*
> *And should be cherished and valued*
>
> *And not be wasted or abused*
> *So please be careful and please be smart*
> *And please don't let your love fall apart*
> *By what you do in the park so green*
> *Or what you say in the air so clean*
>
> *Remember your parents and remember your belief*

And remember your values and remember your destiny
And remember your chaperon who is here for you
To help you stay safe and stay true"

Tunde and Amina heard Bunmi's words and felt a shock of fear in their hearts. They realised they were about to do something wrong and disrespectful. So, each got up from the grass and looked away from each other. They felt embarrassed about their behaviour.

THEY ALSO HEARD BUNMI'S words and felt a hint of gratitude in their hearts because they could see she was right and that she cared for them. Bunmi had saved them from making a mistake that could ruin their relationship. She reminded them of what was important in life.

Once again, they were very sorry for what they were about to do.

"I'm sorry, Bunmi, I feel I've let myself down when I should have known better," Tunde said.

"Me too! I'm so sorry, Aunty. I'll be more careful from now on."

Bunmi smiled at them and forgave them.

"It's okay guys. To be completely honest, I feel so pleased that you both listened to me."

They all hugged each other and left the park.

The youths learned a valuable lesson that day: Love is not just about feelings or actions; it's also about choices and the consequences that come with them. They made a good choice that night by listening to their attendant and respecting themselves, which helped them avoid the terrible consequence of losing their moral character. Tunde and Amina resolved to strengthen their relationship and to trust and support each other. That experience made them to be more mature and responsible. They were still in love and they were proud of it.

THE FISH, A MARRIAGE, AND THE BABY

Finally, there was a wedding of love as Tunde and Amina became husband and wife and fulfilled their dreams. Then, welcome to the family of joy after the couple welcomed their son Gbenga into the world. Their love was a classic affair; a romantic story that began with a salmon and ended with a blessed family.

Amina and Tunde finished their education and soon started their careers. Amina had graduated from the medicine college and became a doctor at a local hospital, and Tunde became an engineer at a multinational company in Ikeja. Each of them was now enjoying a wonderful career, but happier and more successful in love. The youngsters had been dating for four years, and during all that time they had respected each other's boundaries and values and had maintained good morality, thanks to the more than one chaperon who helped them. But they finally came of age and had chosen the right time to get married and perhaps start a family. They informed their parents of their decision and promptly received their blessing. They planned to follow the Yoruba traditional marriage rites, which consisted of three stages: the introduction, the engagement, and the reception.

The introduction was the first part, where the families of the bride and groom met for the first time to exchange greetings, gifts, and well wishes. At this intro meeting, they also discussed the details of the wedding, such as the date, the venue, the budget, and the guest list.

The engagement was the second step, where the bride and groom formally accepted each other as husband and wife, wearing colourful and elegant outfits that matched their personalities and preferences. In some sections of the community, the couple also exchanged rings, vows, and kisses at this event.

The reception was the third stage, where the bride and groom celebrated their union with their families, friends, and well-wishers. Delicious food, refreshing drinks, and other delicacies were made available and everybody danced to lively music before the newlyweds received congratulations, along with blessings and gifts.

That day, Amina and Tunde had a wonderful wedding that was fully celebrated with lots of love and happiness. They had waited a long time for it and showed their deep gratitude to their parents for their support and guidance and for raising them well. They soon started life as a young couple, full of hope and optimism for the future. A few days later, after their honeymoon, they moved into a cosy apartment that was close to their workplaces. They then decorated the residence with their personal touches to make it into a comfortable home before deciding to have children after two years of marriage.

They had a baby boy and named him Gbenga, which means 'lift, elevate,' a common short form of Olugbenga, which means "God is great" in Yoruba. The new parents chose this name because they believed that God had been great to them in every way ever since their first meeting at the Agege market years earlier. Gbenga, who was welcomed with love and gratitude, turned out to be a handsome and happy little chap who possessed his father's smile and his mother's eyes.

Gbenga became a blessing, a reward for their decision to remain clean and chaste during their teen relationship. Amina and Tunde lived happily ever after as a family of three. From time to time, they looked back at their journey from meeting at the market to becoming parents of Olugbenga. It was now their turn to look forward to a wonderful future of growing old together as husband and wife; just like their parents.

Tunde and Amina hoped that their little boy Gbenga would grow up one day, find love, and allow a chaperon to guide him and his girl in the way of moral purity.

GRANDPARENTS AND SCHOOLING

"Welcome to the world, Gbenga. You're our miracle and our joy," Papa said, and Mama then added, "You're our son, Gbenga. You're our treasure and our pride." His parents loved the little boy so much.

Growing up, Gbenga was a happy and curious child who explored and learned new things, a sweet little chap who loved to help and share with others. He had the best of both worlds: his parents' love and his grandparents' support. His grandparents, Shola and Tola, as well as Bola and Latifa, lived not far away and visited the young family often to help with taking care of him, teaching him, and playing with him. They also helped his parents with household chores and were always there for them when they needed support.

Oh, all four grandparents loved Gbenga as their own and spoiled him with treats and stories. During some of those storytelling sessions, they taught him about their culture and traditions, as well as teaching the little boy how to be respectful, honest, and generous. Gbenga enjoyed spending time with them and learning from them; that's why he listened to and obeyed his father and mother in everything they asked of him, and everybody regarded him as a good boy who brought joy to his family.

When it was time for Gbenga to go to school, his parents enrolled him in a local school that had a good reputation for academic excellence, moral values, and extracurricular activities, because they wanted to prepare him for the future. Although the boy was excited, he was also nervous about going to school and often wondered what it would be like to meet new people, learn new things, and do new things away from home. He hoped to make friends, do well in his studies, and have fun pursuing his hobbies. Gbenga became a smart boy who had a lot of potential.

On his first day, Gbenga met his headteacher, Mrs Ojo, who welcomed him warmly and introduced him to the class. Mrs Ojo was a friendly woman who loved teaching children and making them feel comfortable. She told Gbenga he was in grade one, which meant he was six years old. She said that he would learn many things this year, such as reading, writing, math, science, art, music, sports, etc. Mrs Ojo also assured him he would make many friends as there were many nice little lads in his grade that year.

Gbenga liked Mrs Ojo very much for her welcome and introduction.

GBENGA MEETS A GIRL

There was a new girl in his neighbourhood whom Gbenga met on the way to school one day; her name was Bisi, and she had recently moved in with her aunt. She was also going to the same school as him, but she did not know anyone there yet, and this made Bisi nervous. Gbenga saw her walking alone on the street, carrying a backpack and a lunch box, looking lost and confused, as if she did not know where to go. The little boy felt sorry for her and helped her. So, he approached her with a smile and said hello and introduced himself, but she gazed at him and didn't know what to say. Still, he asked her name and told her he was going to the same school as her because their uniform was the same. Gbenga offered to walk with her.

"Hello, I'm Gbenga. What's your name?"

"Nice to meet you, Gbenga. I'm Bisi.

"Nice to meet you too, Bisi. Are you new here?"

"Yes, I just moved in with my aunt. She lives on the next street."

"Oh, I see. Do you like it here?"

"It's okay, I guess. It's very different from where I used to live."

"Where did you used to live?"

"I used to live in Port Harcourt; it's big and busy there."

"Wow, that sounds exciting. Why did you move here?"

"My parents had to go abroad for work. From what I heard, it could be an excellent opportunity for them. They said they would come back soon."

"I'm so sorry. That must be hard for you."

"It is. I miss them a lot. And I miss my friends, too."

"I can understand. I would miss my parents and friends too if I had to move away from them."

"Thank you for understanding."

"You're welcome. Hey, do you know where our school is?"

"No, I don't. I've never been there before."

"Well, don't worry. I'll show you the way. It's not far from here."

"Really? Thank you so much. You're very kind."

"You're welcome. Come on, let's go," Gbenga said.

He took her hand and led her to the school and showed her the gate, the office, the classrooms, the library, the playground, and the cafeteria. He explained the rules, the schedule, the teachers, and the subjects. Gbenga later introduced her to his friends, who welcomed her warmly and invited her to join them at play. He was delighted to find out that they also assigned her to his class, which made him surprised.

From then on, they played together during school breaks and sometimes after school.

DIFFERENT TEACHERS, DIFFERENT SUBJECTS

One day, Gbenga and Bisi walked into a new classroom and saw that it was filled with desks and chairs. There was a chalkboard at the front of the room and a teacher's desk in the corner. Moments later, the teacher walked in and introduced herself as Mrs Johnson, and she was going to be their maths teacher for the year.

"Good morning, class," she said. "My name is Mrs Johnson and I'm going to be your maths teacher this year."

The class said good morning back to her.

Numbers

Mrs Johnson started the lesson by talking about numbers. She explained that numbers were used to count things and that they could be added, subtracted, multiplied, or divided.

She wrote some numbers on the board and asked the class what they were.

"Two," Gbenga said.

"Three," Bisi said.

"Very good," Mrs Johnson said. "Now, can anyone tell me what happens when you add two and three together?"

Gbenga raised his hand. "You get five," he said.

"Excellent," Mrs Johnson said.

Shapes

In the next lesson, Mrs Johnson taught the class a lot about shapes; explaining that shapes were all around us and that they could be described by their sides and angles.

She drew some shapes on the board and asked the class what they were.

"A square," Gbenga said.

"A triangle," Bisi said.

"Very good," Mrs Johnson said. "Now, can one of you tell me how many sides a square has?"

"Four," Chinyere said.

"Brilliant," Mrs Johnson said.

Fractions

When the class assembled for their next maths lesson the following day, Mrs Johnson told them she was going to teach them about fractions and she informed the class that fractions were used to define parts of a whole. After that, the teacher sketched a few fractions on the blackboard and asked the kids what they were.

"One-half," Taribo said.

"One-third," Amaka said.

"Wow, you kids are very intelligent. Now, can anyone tell me what happens when you add one-half and one-third together?"

Bisi raised her hand. "You get five-sixths."

"Well done!"

Decimals

Next, she taught the class about decimals. "We use decimals to describe parts of a whole that are less than one," she explained. Afterwards, she wrote some examples of decimals on the board and asked the class to explain what she wrote.

"Zero point five," said Gbenga.

"Zero point seven-five," Bisi added.

"Thanks to both of you. Now, can anyone tell us what happens when you add zero point five and zero point seven-five together?"

Gbenga raised his hand. "You get one point two-five," he said. "Good answer."

From that day on, Gbenga and Bisi loved Maths even more than before because their Maths teachers made the lessons very enjoyable, and the kids found true happiness in learning new things every day at St Mary's Academy in Ikeja!

THE IMPORTANCE
OF POETRY

Gbenga and Bisi still lived in the city of Ikeja with their families. They both attended the same school and were in the same class, and were excited to start their new lives in this bustling part of Lagos city. The school was called St. Mary's Academy, and it was one of the best because the teachers were all dedicated and the students were eager to learn.

On the first day of the new school year, Gbenga and Bisi arrived in their new classroom and chose their desks and chairs. There was the teacher's desk in the corner, and soon she walked in and introduced herself as Mrs Tunji, and told them she was going to be their English teacher for the year.

"Good morning, class. Welcome to St. Mary's Academy. I hope you are all ready to learn and have fun this year. We're going to spend a lot of time together because I will be teaching you poetry as part of your English lessons. It is a very important subject because it helps you communicate with others, express yourself, and understand different cultures. Also, poetry is a beautiful subject that has many forms, such as literature, short stories, plays, and rhymes. Today, we are going to learn more about poetry. Now, can anyone tell me what poetry is?"

The class was silent for a moment. No one seemed to know the answer. Gbenga raised his hand hesitantly.

"Yes, Gbenga?"

"Is poetry when you rhyme words at the end of sentences?" Gbenga asked.

"That's a good guess, Gbenga, but not quite. Poetry is more than just rhyming words. Poetry is a form of literature that uses language to arouse emotion. Poets use words to create images, sounds, feelings, and meanings that are not always obvious or literal. We can write poetry in many ways, such as using rhyme, rhythm, meter, simile, metaphor, personification, and many more. Poetry can also be written in different forms, such as sonnets, haikus, limericks, free verse, ballads, odes, elegies, and many more." Mrs Tunji explained.

She wrote some examples of poetry on the board:

- *Shall I compare thee to a summer's day?*
- *I wandered lonely as a cloud*
- *The owl and the pussycat went to sea*
- *Do not go gentle into that good night*

"Can anyone tell me what these lines mean? What emotions do they convey? What poetic devices do they use?" Mrs Tunji asked.

Bisi raised her hand eagerly.

"Yes, Bisi?"

"The first line is from a sonnet by William Shakespeare. He is comparing his lover to a summer's day because he thinks she is beautiful and warm. He uses a simile to make the comparison." Bisi answered.

"Very good, Bisi. You are right. That line is from Sonnet 18 by William Shakespeare. He uses a simile to compare his lover to a summer's day using the word 'like' or 'as'. A simile is a figure of speech that compares two things that are different but have something in common." Mrs Tunji said.

She wrote 'simile' on the board and gave some more examples:

- *She is as sweet as honey*
- *He runs like the wind*
- *Her eyes sparkle like stars*

"Question for all of you – Who can tell me something about the second line?"

Uche raised his hand.

"Yes?" Mrs Tunji said.

"The second line is from a poem by William Wordsworth. He is describing how he feels when he sees daffodils in the field."

"That's wonderful. You are right. That line is from I Wandered Lonely as a Cloud by William Wordsworth. He uses a metaphor to compare himself to a cloud without using the words 'like' or 'as.' A metaphor is another figure of speech that compares two things that are different but have something in common."

She wrote 'metaphor' on the board and gave some more examples:

- *Life is a roller coaster*
- *He is a lion in battle*
- *Her voice is music to my ears*

"Okay, who among you could tell me about the third line?" Mrs Tunji asked.

Shola raised her hand.

"Yes?"

"The third line is by Edward Lear. He uses rhyme to make the words sound similar at the end of each line." The girl said.

"VERY GOOD. YOU ARE right. That line is from The Owl and the Pussycat. He uses rhyme to create a pattern of sounds. So, rhyme is a sound device that makes poetry more musical and memorable."

Mrs Tunji then wrote 'rhyme' on the board and gave some more examples:

• *Humpty Dumpty sat on a wall*

- *Jack and Jill went up the hill*
- *Twinkle, twinkle, little star*

Afterwards, she asked the class, "Can anyone tell me about the last line?"

A boy raised his hand.

"Yes?"

"The last line is from a poem by Dylan Thomas. He is talking about his father, who is dying. He uses repetition to emphasise his message."

"Very good. You are right. That line is from Do Not Go Gentle into That Good Night. He uses repetition to repeat words or phrases for effect. Repetition is another sound device that makes poetry more powerful and expressive."

She wrote 'repetition' on the board and gave some more examples:

- *Never, never, never give up*
- *Let it snow, let it snow, let it snow*
- *I have a dream, I have a dream, I have a dream*

In the end, Mrs Tunji smiled and clapped her hands for the class and said, "Wow, you are all very smart and observant. You have learned a lot about poetry today. Poetry is a wonderful way to express yourself and appreciate the beauty of language. I hope you will enjoy reading and writing poetry this year. For your homework, I want you to write your own poem using any of the poetic devices we learned today. You can write about anything you want, as long as it is appropriate for school. You can use rhyme, simile, metaphor, repetition, or any other device you like. Be creative and have fun. I look forward to reading your poems tomorrow."

The class, too, cheered and clapped their hands; they were excited about the idea of writing their own poems. Gbenga and Bisi looked at each other and smiled because they already had a lot of ideas in their minds and couldn't wait to get home and start writing.

The next day, she collected the poems and read them aloud in class, praising each student for their effort and creativity. Their hard work impressed the teacher and gave them all good grades. Gbenga and Bisi were especially proud of their poems. They had written about their families, friends, and dreams, and used different poetic devices to make theirs interesting and meaningful. They had expressed themselves in a way they had never done before; because they had now discovered the joy of poetry.

Sonnets

The following week, Mrs Tunji taught the class about sonnets and explained that they were a type of poem that had 14 lines and followed a specific rhyme scheme. After writing some examples on the board, the teacher asked them what they thought it meant.

"Shall I compare thee to a summer's day?
Thou art more lovely and more temperate:
Rough winds do shake the darling buds of May,
And summer's lease hath all too short a date."

Bisi raised her hand. "It means that love is more beautiful than nature."

"That's good. You're doing very well. Please keep up your hard work."

Bisi and Gbenga continued to do well in poetry because they put their heart into it.

INFORMATION TECHNOLOGY

"**G**ood morning, children, and welcome to St. Mary's. I know you are all ready to learn and have fun this school year. By the way, my name is Ms Chukwu and I will be teaching you Information Technology. Today, we are going to learn the basics of computers and information technology. Can anyone tell me what computers are?" Ms Chukwu asked.

The class was silent for a moment. No one seemed to know the answer. Amaka raised her hand hesitantly.

"Yes, Amaka?" Ms Chukwu said.

"Are computers those machines used to play games and watch videos?" Bisi asked.

"That's a good guess, Amaka, but not quite. Computers are more than just machines that we use for entertainment. They're electronic devices that process data and perform calculations and can store, retrieve, manipulate, and communicate information. Computers can do many things that humans can do, but faster and more accurately."

She wrote some examples of computers on the board:

- *Tablet*
- *Laptop*
- *Desktop*
- *Smartphone*

"Who would like to tell me what these devices are, what they have in common, and what their differences are?"

Gbenga was the first to raise his hand, and he did so eagerly.

"Okay, it looks like Gbenga has the answers. Please go ahead, Gbenga."

"All of them are computers that can run programs and connect to the internet."

"That's correct. Anything else?"

"Yes, they're different in their size and shape," Gbenga answered.

"VERY GOOD, GBENGA. You are right. These devices are all examples of computers that we use every day. They can run programs or applications that allow us to do different tasks, such as writing documents, sending emails, browsing websites, playing games, listening to music, taking pictures, making calls, and many more. These machines can also connect to the internet or a network of computers that share information around the world. Each is different in its size, shape, and features, depending on its purpose and design." Ms Chukwu told the children. She wrote 'programs' and 'internet' on the board and gave some more examples:

- *Facebook*
- *WhatsApp*
- *Microsoft Word*
- *Google Chrome*

"Can anyone tell me what these names are? What do they do? How do they work?"

Another student raised his hand.

"Yes?" Ms Chukwu said.

"These names are examples of programs or applications that run on computers. Microsoft Word is a program that lets you write documents like letters or essays. Google Chrome is a program that lets you browse websites like Wikipedia or YouTube. Facebook is a program that lets you socialise with friends online by posting messages or pictures. WhatsApp is a program that lets you chat or call with your contacts using your phone number."

"Very good. These names are examples of programs or applications that run on computers.

"Teacher, what are applications?" A student asked.

"Applications are sets of instructions that tell computers what to do. They can be installed on your computer or accessed through the internet using a web browser like Google Chrome. Programs or applications can help you do various tasks using your computer." Ms Chukwu said.

She wrote 'web browser' on the board and gave some more examples:

- *Safari*
- *Opera*
- *Mozilla Firefox*

- *Microsoft Edge*

"Can you kids tell me what these names are?"

A girl raised her hand.

"Yes?"

"These names are examples of browsers or programs that let you visit websites on the internet. They can display web pages or documents that contain text, images, videos, links, and other elements, and are different in their appearance, speed, and features depending on their developer and version."

"Oh, my vinegar! You are right. Where did you learn all this?"

"My dad is an IT engineer."

"Ah, that explains a lot. Now, also remember that websites are collections of web pages that are hosted on servers or computers that store and deliver information over the Internet. Websites can provide information, entertainment, education, commerce, and many other services. You can access them by typing their address or URL in the web browser's address bar or by clicking on links that point to them."

She then wrote 'website' and 'URL' on the blackboard and gave the children some more examples:

- *https://www.code.org/*
- *https://www.amazon.com/*
- *https://www.bbc.com/news*
- *https://www.nasa.gov/kidsclub/index.html*

"What are these, and how do they work?"

A boy raised his hand and Ms Chukwu asked him to go ahead.

"These names are examples of URLs or addresses of websites on the internet. They mean that they are using a protocol or a set of rules for communication called HTTPS, which stands for Hypertext Transfer Protocol Secure. They also have a domain name or a name that identifies the website, such as BBC, NASA, or Amazon."

"That's great, well done! Please also note that these URLs may also have a path or a specific location within the website, such as news, kids' club, or index. They work by sending a request to the server that hosts the website and receiving a response with the web page content. This means that URLs are unique identifiers that tell web browsers where to find websites on the internet. They consist of different parts that specify the protocol, domain name, path, and other parameters of the website. URLs can be typed in the web browser's address bar or copied and pasted from other sources."

At the end of the lesson, the teacher smiled and commended the class for making the lesson enjoyable through their participation.

"Did you learn something about computers and information technology today?"

"Yes, miss!"

"Great! Computers and information technology are very important in our modern society because they help us do many things quicker and better. Even though you are all little children, you still need to learn the basics of computers so that you can use them effectively and responsibly. We will enjoy learning more about computers and information technology this year. For your homework, I want you to visit one of these websites using your computer or smartphone and explore their content. You can choose any website you like, as long as it is suitable and safe. You can learn about news, science, shopping, coding, or anything else that interests you. Write a summary of what you learned and what you liked or disliked about the website. Be honest and creative. I look forward to reading what you wrote tomorrow."

AGRICULTURAL SCIENCE

"**G**ood morning, class; I am Mrs Duru and I will be teaching you different subjects. One of the subjects we will learn this year is agriculture and farming. What is agriculture?"

The class was silent for a moment. No one seemed to know the answer. A boy raised his hand hesitantly.

"Yes, John?"

"Is agriculture when you grow rice or maize?"

"Well done for trying, John. To add to that, agriculture and farming are more than just growing crops or raising animals. Agriculture is the science and practice of cultivating plants and animals for food, fibre, fuel, medicine, and other products that benefit humans. Farming is a type of agriculture that involves managing land, water, soil, plants, and animals to produce food and other goods."

After saying that, she wrote some examples of agriculture and farming on the board:

- *Aquaculture*
- *Horticulture*
- *Crop production*
- *Animal husbandry*

"What do these terms mean?"

"Yes, Bisi?" Mrs Duru said.

"Crop production is when you grow plants that can be harvested for food or other uses, like wheat, cotton, or sugarcane. Animal husbandry is when you breed and care for animals that can provide meat, milk, eggs, wool, or leather, like pigs, goats, or sheep. Aquaculture is when you farm fish or other aquatic organisms in ponds, tanks, or cages, like tilapia, catfish, or seaweed. Horticulture is when you cultivate fruits, vegetables, flowers, or ornamental plants in gardens, greenhouses, or nurseries, like oranges, tomatoes, roses, or bonsai."

Bisi's answer impressed the teacher.

"VERY GOOD, BISI. YOU are right. These terms are examples of different types of agriculture and farming that produce different products for different purposes. They have in common that they all involve growing or raising living things that need water, sunlight, nutrients, and care. They are different in their methods, techniques, tools, and environments depending on their goals and challenges."

She wrote 'water', 'sunlight', 'nutrients', and 'care' on the board and gave some more examples:

- *Irrigation*
- *Fertiliser*
- *Pesticide*
- *Vaccine*

"These words are examples of things that farmers often use to help their crops or animals grow better and healthier. Irrigation is when you supply water to your plants or animals using pipes, sprinklers, or canals. Fertiliser is when you add nutrients to your soil or water to make your plants or animals grow faster and stronger. Pesticide is when you use chemicals or natural substances to kill pests or diseases that can harm your plants or animals. A vaccine is when you inject your animals with a weakened or dead form of a virus or bacteria to protect them from getting sick. Irrigation, manure, pesticides, and vaccines are all ways of providing water, sunlight, nutrients, and care for your plants or animals. They can improve the quantity and quality of your products, but they can also have some disadvantages or risks if not used properly."

She wrote 'quantity', 'quality', 'drawbacks', and 'risks' on the board and gave some more examples:

- *Yield*
- *Taste*
- *Pollution*
- *Resistance*

"These words are examples of the outcomes or consequences of agriculture and farming. Yield is the amount of product that you get from your plants or animals, like how many kilograms of rice or litres of milk. Taste is the flavour or quality of your product that makes it appealing or enjoyable to eat or drink, like how sweet or sour your oranges or yoghurts are. Pollution is the damage to the environment by your farming activities, like how your manure or pesticide can run off into the water or air and harm other living things. Resistance is the ability of your pests or diseases to survive or overcome your pesticide or vaccine, like how some insects or germs can become immune or stronger and harder to kill. Farmers have to balance these factors and make decisions that are good for themselves, their customers, and their environment." Mrs Duru said.

AFTERWARDS, SHE SAID a well done to the kids and gave them things to work on at home.

"Agriculture and farming are very important in our society because they provide us with food and other products that we need and want. Even little children like you need to learn the basics of agriculture and farming so that they can appreciate where their food comes from, how it is produced, and what impact it has on the world. For your homework, draw a picture of a farm that you would like to visit or work on using any type of agriculture or farming that we learned today. You can draw any plants or animals that you like. You can also label your picture with the names of the things that you drew. Be imaginative; have fun! See you tomorrow."

The next day, Mrs Duru collected their pictures and displayed them on the wall. She praised each student for their effort and imagination. She was impressed by their pictures and gave them all good grades. Gbenga and Bisi had drawn different farms and different types of farming. They had drawn crops like maize, cassava, cocoa, and palm oil; animals like cows, chickens, fish, and snails; tools like tractors, ploughs, nets, and cages; products like bread, cheese, oil, and chocolate; and problems like drought, flood, pests, and diseases. They had labelled their pictures with the names of the things that they drew.

PHYSICAL EDUCATION

Mr Ekwem was a young and energetic teacher who loved sports and fitness and always encouraged his students to be active and healthy and taught them about the benefits of physical education for their bodies, minds, and society. He made his lessons fun and interactive and often asked his students to participate in various activities and games. The kids loved his sessions.

One day, Mr Ekwem walked into the classroom with a big smile on his face and told the class that they were going to learn about physical education and its impact on society.

"Today we are going to talk about PE. PE is when we do physical activities that help us improve our health, fitness, and skills. It also helps us develop social and emotional skills that are important for our relationships with others. PE is not only good for us as individuals, but also for our families and society. Can anyone tell me how PE can benefit our families?"

The students thought for a while. Then one of them raised his hand.

"Yes, Chidi?"

Chidi said, "PE can benefit our families by making us happier and closer."

"How so?" Mr Ekwem asked.

"Well, when we do PE with our families, we can have fun together, share our feelings, and support each other. We can also learn from each other and appreciate each other's strengths and weaknesses."

"That's very true, Chidi. PE can strengthen our family bonds and make us happier. Thank you for sharing that."

Mr Ekwem then asked another question.

"How about society? How can PE benefit our society?"

The students thought harder this time. Then one of them raised her hand.

"Yes, Ngozi?"

"PE can benefit our society by making us healthier and more productive."

"Okay, please tell us more."

"Well, when we do PE regularly, we can prevent diseases, improve our immunity, and reduce stress. We can also boost our energy, concentration, and creativity. This can make us more productive at work, school, or whatever we do."

"That's very true, Ngozi. PE can improve our physical and mental well-being and make us more productive members of society. Thank you for your comments."

Because they loved the class so much, the kids said in unison, "Thank you, Mr Ekwem!"

Mr Ekwem smiled and said, "You're very welcome, class. Now that you know how important PE is for you, your families, and your society, I hope you will continue to practise it regularly and enjoy it. And to help you do that, I have prepared a special activity for you today."

The students gasped in excitement.

"What is it?" they asked eagerly.

"You'll see soon enough. But first, let me tell you what you need to do. You need to form groups of four or five people each. Then you need to pick a sport or a game that you want to play with your group.

It can be anything you like: football, basketball, volleyball, badminton, tennis, table tennis, chess... anything!"

The students cheered louder.

"Yay!" they exclaimed.

Mr Ekwem continued.

"Once you have picked your sport or game, you need to write down the name of it on a piece of paper. Then you need to write down three reasons why you like it or why it is good for you. For example: I like football because it is fun / it improves my coordination / it teaches me teamwork."

The students nodded in understanding.

"Got it!" they said.

"Good! Then you need to give me your paper with your sport or game name and your reasons. I will collect them and put them in a hat. Then I will draw one paper randomly and announce the sport or game that we will all play today. Sounds good?"

The students nodded and clapped again.

"Sounds great!" they said.

"Alright then, let's get started! Form your groups and pick your sport or game. You have 10 minutes to do that. Go!"

The students quickly formed their groups and started discussing their sport or game choices. Gbenga and Bisi joined the same group with two other friends, Uche and Fatima. They decided to pick badminton as their sport.

THEY WROTE DOWN THEIR sports names and their reasons on
a piece of paper. This is what they wrote:

We like badminton because:

- *It is fun and easy to play.*
- *It improves our speed, agility, and reflexes.*
- *It helps us make new friends and socialise.*

They gave their paper to the teacher, who put it in his hat along with the other papers from the other groups. He then shook the hat and drew one piece of paper randomly.

He opened the paper and read it out loud.

"And the sport or game that we will play today is... badminton!"

Gbenga, Bisi, Uche, and Fatima cheered in joy.

"Yay! We won!"

The other students also clapped and congratulated them.

"Good job!" they said.

"Congratulations to Gbenga, Bisi, Uche, and Fatima for picking badminton as our sport today. Badminton is a great sport that has many benefits for our health, fitness, and skills. It is also a lot of fun to play with others. Are you ready to play some badminton?"

"Yes!" the students nodded eagerly.

"Great! Then let's go to the gymnasium where we have some badminton courts set up for us. Follow me!"

The coach led the students to the gymnasium, where they saw several badminton nets, rackets, and shuttlecocks waiting for them. After dividing the students into teams of two and assigning them to different courts, the teacher gave them some instructions on how to play badminton and some safety tips. He then blew his whistle and started the game.

The students had a blast playing badminton with their friends. Each enjoyed hitting the shuttlecock back and forth over the net, trying to score points or prevent their opponents from scoring. Many also enjoyed cheering for their teammates or other teams, making new friends or strengthening old ones. They laughed, sweated, and learned a lot from the game.

The teacher watched them play with a smile on his face and was happy to see his students having fun and being active. He knew that they were not only playing a sport but also learning valuable lessons about physical education and its impact on their lives. He thought to himself:

"This is what PE is all about."

ART AND CRAFT

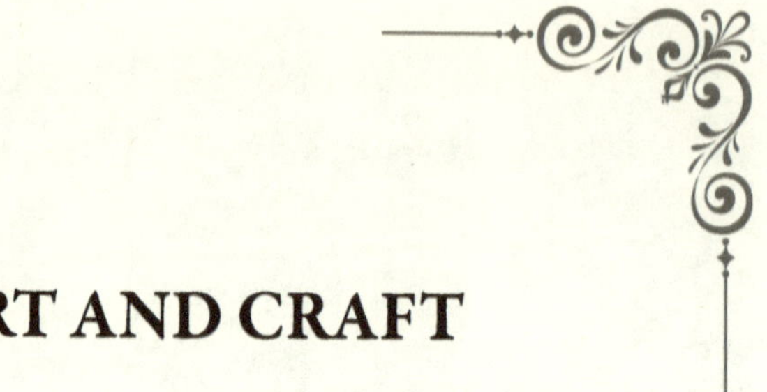

Gbenga and Bisi liked their school, especially their art and crafts teacher, Mr Ekwem.

Mr Ekwem was a young and creative man who loved art and craft. He always encouraged his students to be artistic and expressive and taught them about the benefits of art and craft for their minds, hearts, and society. He made his lessons fun and interactive and often asked his students to take part in various projects and activities.

The next day, Mr Ekwem told his class that they were going to learn a new subject and its impact on individuals, families, and society.

"Good morning, class! Today we are going to talk about arts and crafts, or A&C for short. Can anyone tell me what A&C is all about?"

A few hands went up in the air.

"It's great to see so many hands raised, but let's hear from Gbenga."

Gbenga stood up and answered confidently, "A&C is when we make things with our hands and our imagination."

"Excellent, Gbenga. A&C is also when we create things using different materials, tools, techniques, and ideas. A&C also helps us communicate our emotions, opinions, and messages through our creations."

He continued.

"Art & Craft is not only good for us as individuals, but also for our families and society. With A&C, we can have fun together, share our feelings, and support each other. We can also learn from each other and appreciate each other's talents and creativity. A&C broadens our horizons and makes us more aware of our surroundings and ourselves."

He then concluded the lesson, "Now that you know how important A&C is for you, your families, and your society, I hope you will continue to practise it regularly and enjoy it. And to help you do that, I have prepared a special activity for you today. But first, let me tell you what you need to do. You need to form groups of four or five people each. Then you need to pick a theme or a topic that you want to make an art or craft project about with your group. It can be anything you like: animals, plants, people, places, events... anything!"

The students cheered, "Yay!"

"Once you have picked your theme or topic, you need to write it on a piece of paper. Then you need to write three reasons why you chose it or why it is interesting to you. For example, I chose animals because they are cute / they are diverse / they teach us about nature."

The students nodded, "Got it!"

"Good! Give me your paper with your theme or topic name and your reasons. As usual, I'll draw one randomly and announce the topic that we will all make an art or craft project about today. Sounds good?"

"Sounds great!" they said.

"Alright then, let's get started! Form your groups and pick your theme or topic. You have 5 minutes to do that."

The students quickly formed their groups and wrote down their theme name and their reasons on a piece of paper. We chose plants because:

- *They are beneficial.*
- *They are beautiful and colourful.*
- *They help us learn about science and art.*

They submitted theirs and he put it in the hat with the others before drawing out one randomly. He opened it and read it out loud.

"And the theme that we will make an art or craft project about today is... plants!"

Gbenga, Bisi, Chidi, and Fatima cheered in joy.

"Yay! We won again!" they shouted.

Learning can be fun! When you work hard and put your heart into it, you'll find joy in learning new things!

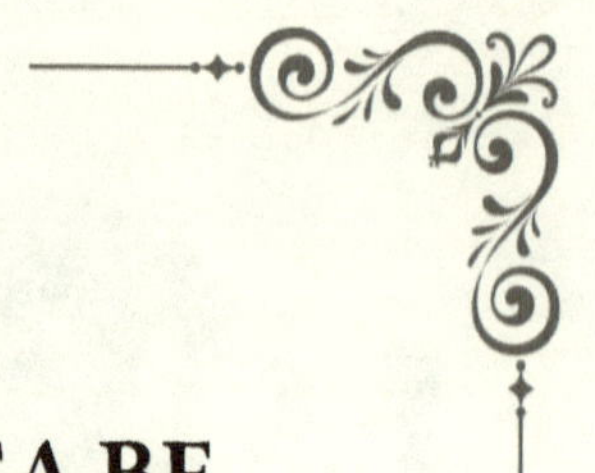

MIGHT GBENGA BE
FALLING IN LOVE?

The kids were growing very fast and learning a lot at school, and could now write some interesting poems and essays. They had also become close friends.

One day, as they were walking through a park after school, Gbenga stopped in front of a beautiful tree.

"This is my favourite tree, it's called an Iroko tree."

"It's beautiful," Bisi agreed.

Gbenga smiled at her. "I wrote a poem about this tree."

"Really?"

"Yep! Would you like to hear it?"

She nodded eagerly. Encouraged, Gbenga cleared his throat and began:

In this land of ours,
Where trees grow so tall,
I see your beauty shining,
Like the morning dewfall.

Your heart is like music,
That fills me with joy,
And I know that with you,
I'll never be nervous.

Bisi was so moved by Gbenga's poem that she wrote one for him too:

In this land of ours,
Where love grows so true,
I see your heart shining,
Like the morning dew.

Your love is like sunshine,
That warms me inside,
And I know that with you,
I'll always be cool.

The End!

CONCLUSION

Some lessons for the youths who are going to read this romance novel are:

- Falling in love is beautiful! However, it can also create powerful emotions that can inspire and motivate people to achieve their dreams and goals. Love and affection bring joy and happiness to people's lives, making them better persons.

- Love, especially romantic love, is also a sacred and precious gift that should be respected and not be abused or taken for granted. It should not be based on physical desire or selfishness, but rather on trust and commitment.

- Love requires patience as well as wisdom; that's why it's never something that can be rushed or forced, but must be allowed to develop over time. It must be nurtured and protected.

- Romantic love requires communication and understanding. It is not something that can be assumed or guessed but needs to be expressed and shared.

- Love requires lots of compromise due to the challenges that come with it; love is not easy or perfect, it tests people's faith and character. To receive it, you must first give it.

- Finally, true love isn't cheap or casual. It involves respect and loyalty and must be faithful and true.

These are some of the lessons and morals that Amina and Tunde learned from their teen romance, and they hope to share them with other youths who are going to read their novel. They hope to inspire them to love wisely and to enjoy the rewards of loyal, undiluted love in their lives.

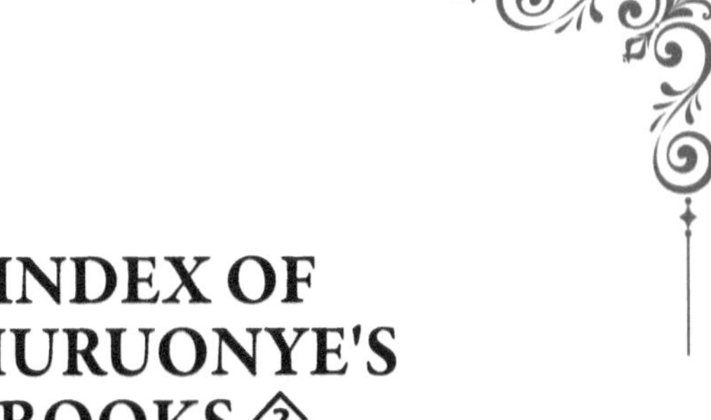

INDEX OF
AHURUONYE'S
BOOKS

Gratitude Journal – 2022
The Power of Gratitude – 2022
My Dogbook – 2022
Meditation Diary – 2022
Happyville – 2023
Stinky and The Dung Beetle – 2023
Oh, What A Mars! 2023
The Gull Who Must Be Obeyed – 2023
The Groccolli PictureLand ChatBook – 2023
Trillion-Her – 2023
Finding Love in Cahersiveen – 2023

AUTHOR BIOGRAPHY

Ahuruonye was born in Aba, Nigeria, and has spent much of his adult life in Europe. His father was Mr Friday Enwereji Ahuruonye; one of the many children of a traditional ruler – Chief Ahuruonye (Nwákà) Ikpefu. His mother was Madam Joy Chinagorom Ahuruonye, daughter of Pa Moses and Madam Elizabeth Ngwaahụ Ihesiulo Nwachukwu in Ahiaba-Ubi, Abia State.

He started his education at Umuikaa Central Primary School soon after the Biafran War and later moved to Mkpuka Community Primary School. After his primary education, Ahuruonye attended St. Ephraim Secondary School, Owerrinta. Ahuruonye subsequently completed his studies at the Dublin Institute of Technology, Ireland. He holds a diploma in fashion design and a University Certificate in Medical Record from DIT (HMI).

Dandy has published several books including a technical work on fashion and designing: "The Shoemaker - Principles and Guide for Professionals." He has also published a host of children's books including: 'Illustrated Children's Stories;' 'Groccoli;' 'Waka;' 'The Good and Ugly Weather Friends;' 'The Eel and Phil in Kill;' 'The Grass Fart in Donegal Bay.' His most prominent work is the 600-page encyclopaedia: The Whispering Poet – An Anthology of Igbo & Other Proverbs.

LAGOS TEENS
and
The Marketplace of Dreams

DANDY AHURUONYE
The Whispering Poet

A Lifetime of Tales from The Whispering Poet
dandyahuruonyebooks@gmail.com

Don't miss out!

Visit the website below and you can sign up to receive emails whenever Dandy Ahuruonye publishes a new book. There's no charge and no obligation.

https://books2read.com/r/B-A-YNSQ-GEAPC

BOOKS 2 READ

Connecting independent readers to independent writers.

Did you love *Lagos Teens and the marketplace of dreams*? Then you should read *The Gull Who Must be Obeyed*[1] by Dandy Ahuruonye!

Welcome to the world of seagulls, where life is full of adventure, danger, and drama. In this book, you will meet some of the most colourful and memorable characters that fly over the coast of Ireland. Some of them are brave and noble, some of them cunning and clever, and the rest are just plain naughty and nasty. But they all have one thing in common: they love to eat!

Meet Gussbol, 'the gull who must be obeyed,' a dominant bird on the coast who acts like the king of the seagulls. He never shares food and will eat anything, even if it's not good for him. One day, he meets his match: Rumi, a younger but powerful gull who challenges him for his throne. Both become enemies, and they fight over everything.

---

1. https://books2read.com/u/bzBdvL

2. https://books2read.com/u/bzBdvL

However, they learn the hard way that sometimes it's better to cooperate than to fight.

Not only Gussbol, but also Gullaign is causing trouble in town. Gullaign likes to pick fights and his favourite target is Mr Beardstone, a fishmonger who lives in a small cottage near the shore. Gullaign steals his food and tries to sabotage his business, but Beardstone is not an easy man to mess with. Seagullora and Guswayne are two clever royals who lead a small group of loyal followers to foil a plot to kidnap and ship all the seagulls to a remote island. They discover those behind this evil scheme and must stop them before it is too late. They use their wits and skills to outsmart their enemies and save their friends.

We'll also meet Bakassi, the notorious 'Gangster Seagull'. Known for his tough demeanour, Bakassi sports a sleek black leather jacket, a flashy gold chain, and sunglasses. His beak bears a scar that only adds to his rugged appearance, and his wing boasts a skull tattoo. Bakassi's favourite pastimes include stealing food, chasing away other birds, and making a ruckus.

Will his fellow seagulls learn to cooperate and foster friendships with him?

The Gull Who Must Be Obeyed is a funny kids' book with witty one-liners and true humour throughout. It features exciting characters that will make you love them or hate them, depending on your point of view. It is a book that will teach your child some valuable lessons about life, friendship, and courage. Meet the seagulls who rule the skies...and cause trouble for everyone else!

So, what are you waiting for? Grab your copy today and join the fun; you won't regret it!

Read more at https://wordpress.com/home/ dandyahuruonye.wordpress.com.

Also by Dandy Ahuruonye

THE WHISPERING POET: An Anthology of Igbo And Other
Proverbs
Grocc-ofly
Reading Glasses for Mama Eagle
The Cute Kids of Madugascar
Nora never gave up
A Fishhook and the Riverboy
Positive Brainwash
Groccolli
The Adventures of Groccolli
Happyville
Oh, What a Mars!
Stinky and The Dung Beetle
The Gull Who Must be Obeyed
THE SHOEMAKER: Principles & Guide for Professionals
The Groccolli Pictureland Chatbook
Finding Love in Cahersiveen
Trillion-Her
Lagos Teens and the marketplace of dreams

Watch for more at https://wordpress.com/home/
dandyahuruonye.wordpress.com.

About the Author

Dandy Ahuruonye has written several books, starting with the widely released novel: 'Long Search for Greener Pastures,' and the technical manual on footwear designing: 'THE SHOEMAKER - Principles & Guide for Professionals,' and 'DESIGNER'S FINGER: A Practical Guide For Shoe Professionals. Dandy has also released a host of children's books including: 'The Grass Fart in Donegal Bay,' 'Waboubou', 'Shokeleke', 'Zinzie,' 'Metu,' 'Laka,' and many others. His biggest work so far is the 600-page cultural encyclopaedia – THE WHISPERING POET: An Anthology of Igbo & Other Proverbs. This book, 'NORA Never Gave Up' adds to his growing list of published books.

Read more at https://dandyahuruonye.wordpress.com/.